AF191216

© 2020 Motte, R.
Kustantaja: BoD – Books on Demand, Helsinki, Suomi
Valmistaja: BoD – Books on Demand, Norderstedt, Saksa
ISBN: 978-952-802-308-1

Silence & Wind chime

Short novels

To 'K'

3.5.2005 – 31.7.2014

I'll always remember you

Stories to read

Road Trip

The Promise

With You

The Rules

Flock

Temptation

Wait

Bunny

Echo

Actress of Self-Hurting Play

Worth Every Dime

It's a Date

Give it a Try

No Reality

Moment of Clarity

Lucid Dream

Road Trip

The Promise

Laughter. It's his laughter that lightened that dark autumn morning. He came from the rainiest place on the whole wide world; yet the sound of his laugh made the whole class room enlightened.

His name was Perry Jones and he came all across the ocean;
from the land of rain and tea.

On the first few weeks I was thin air for him. No one even bothered to introduce us to one-another. It was one party at my friends Hannah's place that changed everything.

"Alright! Is there anyone – And I mean *anyone* who would like to come and play some – ?" Perry's voice shouted from the terrace. I went to the huge living room window and saw people gathering there to play some soccer. As Perry sees me he waves at me to go along with the rest of them. I point at my high heels and he comes in and lifts me up and carries me to the terrace where he places me to sit on the railing of the terrace while he takes of my high heels. I'm so shocked that I can't resist him.

"Shoes off everyone – No hard kicking on the ball, so we won't chop nails!" he commands as he places me down to my feet.
"You are on my team.. That's the one that keeps their shirts on", he tells me with a smug smile.

I honestly suck at soccer. I won't deny it.
But no one seemed to mind it as much as I did, people were just having fun.
Within an hour or so my feet were green.

As we all sat on the grass and ate a pizza that has magically been brought to us outside by Hannah's parents we agree that soccer doesn't quite give the same rush as football, but it was hell of a lot easier to play on the backyard.

I watch Perry writing down something on a piece of paper before he freezes. Then he lifts his gaze on me with a shock.

"I'm so sorry – I don't know your name", he realizes.

"It's Aimee", I tell him with a smile. All the sudden people left and I see flickering lights coming from the living room. Someone has plugged in a video game and people have went there.

"Guess no one likes to play anymore", Perry says as he starts to get up.

"I'm still here", I tell him. I can see a hint of a smile on his cheek. Then his gaze moves a bit and he only nods to someone. I turn around to see group of boys who come over. Some of the boys are older than me, I bet they were from same class as Hannah's boyfriend.

One of them takes me under his arm which makes me super-uncomfortable. I take the hand off within seconds and everyone tells the guy to stop it at once. Perry persuades them for another game and I excuse myself indoors to get away from the guy who seemingly can't keep his hands off me. As I put my heels back on I find the piece of paper Perry had wrote. It said:

Someday – I will take you out Aimee.

xxx-xxx-xxxx

I had never been given numbers from boys before and I was thrilled. Yet after that party we simply started to hang out more often. Nothing major, simple friend gatherings, going to the movies, hanging at the park.. I even sent him text message so he'd got my number; Yet I didn't have the nerve to ask him out myself. So it simply slipped my mind – the possibility.

. . .

Time flied by and soon as I know I was on my late twenties ready to concur the World; even that meant working on a crappy salary at news company.

On my first day there I was shocked to see Perry there.

"Aimee!" he greets me in as we walk the office around while being lead to the meeting room. "Perry!" I greet him back as he says hi to everyone else as well.

"What are you doing here?"

"Working".

"Well that sounds like you" Perry says as he stares at me with unreadable impression.

"Come sit with us – " Perry's friend allures him as he explains how they could do something with that total 'wow'-factor and all.

"I'm sorry, wait a minute Aimee", Perry apologizes. Perry had made his way through all the social steps of new working place by hard work and unbeatable charm and within few years he had become assistant of our travel-columnist.

As he leaves I find myself a seat and attend to the morning meeting only to be given a note from Perry.

"Haven't forgotten my promise"

With You

After the meeting Perry and I settle to go out on a dinner-date after the work on the following Friday. I can't help myself from feeling more or less like thin air while waiting for him. All the others out there were so keenly trying to get Perry's attention and I had nothing – I was a common rock next to a jewel.

For my surprise Perry kept his eyes on me. He showed me his most genuine smile as he walked his way to me.
"I'm sorry that I kept you waiting", Perry apologizes as we walk to his car and opens the door for me.
"It's alright", I tell him back as I get in. Some other girls come to speak to Perry the minute he closes the door.

Perry's impression remains calm and cheerful as he gestures towards me – who's already in the car – to the girls and smiles again before he takes a seat on the driver's side.
"So.. You really want to hang out with me tonight?" I confirm from him.

"I promised you so", he reminds me.

"I didn't actually believe you'd keep that promise.." I admit.

"Why wouldn't I?" he asks back as he glances at me. I found it funny how his curly hair worked it's way against gravity and other laws of nature by it's structure.

"It's been a lifetime when you made that promise", I sigh as my head falls down. All the sudden he pulls my head up with his fingertip.

"I didn't forget you – I am here now, right? So where do you want to go?" Perry speaks.

"I don't know", I say back as I continue, "Anything but Indian or Mexican food for me".

"I don't like *that* spicy foods either", Perry reveals as he tries to think while driving.

"OK. I think I know a place", he declares as he takes vicious looking yet *legal* turns towards the place he had in his mind. I took it as a mental note to rip my own driver's license in two once I'd get my hands to the scissors, because he had such skills that most of us would die for.

Perry parked the car next to the street and took out his wallet for the parking meter.

"This will take a sec", he informs me before he heads out of the car. I turn to look at nice and warm looking restaurant – Not a super official looking one – warm and nice looking one; like I said. I snap out of my thoughts when Perry opens my door.

"Thank you", I stutter. I knew he was a gentleman but to be the sole person to experience it was something unique. We head in to the restaurant and are given a seemingly nice table in the middle, for other tables were taken already.

"Can't win it all I guess", Perry jokes about it, "They have to walk a bit more to their car". As I try to hold my laughter my phone starts ringing.

"I'm so sorry", I apologize from him. He says it's fine, he forgot to mute his phone too and as I'm given an excuse to answer to my phone Perry takes a minute to avoid my error.

"Hi Elle!" I greet my sister.

"Do you need something from the store? I'm still here so – "

"Wait what?" I interrupt her, completely out of what she was talking about.

"I can bring you some veggies if you like.. Make sure Elliot eats them too – ", Elle babbles. I'm getting dizzy by listening to her.

"Elle stop. Just hold on a sec. What are you talking about?!" I demand.

"I couldn't get hold of mom and dad so I'm coming to your place.."

"I'm not at home", I tell her.

"Well I can pick you up – Just tell me where"

"Elle – You're not listening!" I semi-shriek. I hated her for doing these things.

"I'm not at home, because I'm on a date", I explain.

"Oh", Elle states, "Well I haven't got time for that – "

"Well I do, so take care.. And for your information – Again. Mom and Dad are at the concert on the Hall", I remind her before ending the call.

"Were you supposed to be some place else?" Perry asks. I can sense disappointment in his voice.

"No. My older sister is just being.. Her *lovely*-self again", I explain while hinting that I wasn't totally telling it the right way.

"My sibling are also annoying time to times – So how many have you got – I can't remember?"

"Four sisters", I reply, "Three older ones and one younger one.. I can remember you had at least one big brother, right?"

"One big brother, little brother and little sister", Perry answers.

We order our dinner before getting back to our conversation.

"Was something going on with your sister? Something major since she tried to reach your parents – Sorry for listening that much", Perry asks.

"No – Nothing like that. She wanted me to babysit her kids.. She often does that by just leaving them to me, for I'm usually working 'till late so she offers to pick me up and drives me home and what-do-you-know it's late and the kids need to go to bed and then they end up sleeping at my place and my sister gets a nice Friday-out with her boyfriend while I end up babysitting..", I spill it out. For my surprise Perry shares understanding impression.

"Well, that's not the case today – Like you said: You are on a Date", he declares as he raises his water glass. I do the same with laughter.

We continue talking our way through the dinner. For once I was on a date and I wasn't even slightly interested to talk about weather. We had so much more topics to go through. It was like I knew very little about him, yet I had known him forever which made is so easy to be around him.

"Let me guess.. All your older sisters have gotten families of their own and they're trying to make you do the same no matter what you want?"
"Not just my older sisters. My younger sister has family of her own too" I answer.
"So you're the odd-bird of the nest", Perry wonders.
"I.. Just haven't kept it as priority" I lie. For my bad luck I was extremely bad at it. I notice his impression shift a bit, like his impression would have soften more.
"It's not necessarily bad thing, you know?" he points out.
"To my sisters.. It's the end of the world", I joke.

"I can imagine your feelings.. Whenever I visit at home I start to feel bad when I get bombarded with pretty much the same issue", Perry says to me as we split the check, even he pays the dessert for me too.

As we get to the car Perry is about to start it when he freezes.

"How spontaneous are you?" he asks with a mysterious grin on his face.

"That depends", I challenge him.

"How about a Road Trip – Right now?".

"Let's do that", I accept – Part of me is hoping that he was kidding but bigger part of me was sure he wasn't and that made me response to him. Perry starts the engine and steers the car to the street.

"How much time do you have?" he asks then.

"I have nothing on my schedule until Monday"

"Same.. Do you want to spend your weekend with me?" he admits.

"Yes", I answer to his question.

"You better tell your sister that you'll date just got a bit longer", he jokes.

The Rules

" – And if the other one feels even slightly uncomfortable this will be over", Perry promises.

"Sounds reasonable", I agree.

"Even I feel uncomfortable most of the time", he laughs.

"You? Why?" I hear myself ask out of shock. How could someone like him feel uncomfortable?

"I just.. Do so", he answers as he bits his lip a bit, "Do you know any car-games? You know, something we could play while I drive?" he changes the subject.

"Yeah – Quite a lot actually", I reveal.

"Really?" he wonders.

"My dad had money to buy a car.. But it didn't include a radio", I tell him as I remember the time my dad actually bought us the new car.

It was summer time. It was right after my first or second grade. It was hot on that day so me and my older sisters had went to the library to cool ourselves. When we came out our parents and my younger sister were waiting outside, next to this God knows how old car. It was my dad's first car he ever had purchased by himself. He had loaned dozens of them but this one was his and he was so proud of it.

The car was well kept and all and its engine run smoothly – Yet there was no radio in it and the back-doors jammed most of the times along with the trunk.. But it was *ours*.

"So what did you do?" Perry asks, interrupting my memory-lane of my dad's first car.

"Twenty-one questions, I-spy, How many animals; you got extra points of rare ones.." I list.

"Well I just saw a dead raccoon", he informs as he gestures to the back of the road.

"Well I give you half a point, for you didn't know *yet* that the animals need to be alive".

. . .

As the sun sets and the sky gets dark Perry decides to park the car on a resting stop with surveillance and restrooms. We go to refresh ourselves before coming back to the car. To be honest; I was bit surprised to find out that he had an arsenal of bathroom equipments in his car. Perry puts my front seat on a sleeping position while at the same time he climbs to the back of his car and puts down the backseat. He hands me over a blanket and a pillow.

"Do you sleep in your car a lot?" I wonder as I place the pillow under my head. Perry takes of his jacket and shoes before he answers.

"Yeah.. You could say so", he says back while closing the locks.

Flock

After the morning routines we get on the road again. We open our windows and enjoy the slowly warming breeze and the sunlight.

. . .

I was looking at the view while I notice a flock of seagulls been shooed away from a shore by another car. "It's coming right at us!" I shriek in horror. Perry tries to use windshield wipers to scare the birds off, but it's no use – One of the bird first hits on the windshield and then gets sucked under the car because of the momentum of our vehicle.. And that's when we get all soaked by scrapings of the poor bird.

Perry pulls over and I head out of the car instantly throwing up. He does that too.
"Are you alright?" he asks with hoarse sound in his voice. I manage to shook my head as an answer.
"Me neither", Perry admits.
"You two alright there?" unfamiliar voice asks then.

"No – A Seagull flew right at us and then it got sucked under the car and then it got grated inside – ", Perry explains as he shows the car. Man who had stopped to check on us nearly throws up too. The smell and the look were both hideous.

Man is kind enough to give us a ride to the next town while Perry's car was being toed there. While Perry was making clear of the paper work I head onto some second hand shops to get us something to wear. "Car accident – Bird vs. Van. Result: One grated bird", I explain to the worker who's holding her nose. "Just hurry", she begs of me as I scan the shop to find something basic to wear. After that I head to self service laundry where I wash them and dry the, quickly.

I meet Perry on a motel where he has arranged a room for us to clean up ourselves.

Temptation

I place my handbag on one of the two arm chairs on the room.

"Do you want to go to the shower first?" I ask.

"You may go first– I promise I won't peek", he offers.

"I know you won't", I tell him as I take my new set of clothes along with me. I curse myself to the fact that I haven't bought myself a pajamas. So after the shower I settle to wear one of the t-shirts and yoga-pants that I bought.

I'm looking out of the window when Perry comes out from the shower. I can see him perfectly from the reflection, for our room is very dim. I can see that he sees me looking at him so I move my eyes to look back outside. Perry chuckles a bit.

"Oh shush!", I cut him off.

"I saw that", he tells me.

"Can I not look at the person I've spend last thirty hours or so? Especially when he doesn't reek like hell?"

"Hey, watch it, you reeked like hell too you know – I was just gentleman enough not to bring it up", he laughs as he comes over to the window to close the curtains.

Without saying another word Perry kisses me. It was intense sensation that I was unable to resist. As his kisses get more attempting and his breath more intense I can't help to notice his hand under my shirt, finding it's way under my pants –. I take hold of his hands and pause.

"You don't – ", he starts.

"No", I tell him with strong and clear tone. For a minute Perry stares right back at me puzzled by the way I escaped his well cast spell. I can feel myself trembling, like I'd be doing something wrong – That's how strong his spell was.

"Why no?" Perry asks silently. It was like not only his hair that mocked the laws of nature, now the sound of his voice had gained that ability too – It lacked echo.

"I just want to Wait", I answer to him, truthfully.

"So.. You're waiting until – ?" he tries to understand when it hits him. There's something unreadable in him.

"Yes. I want to wait until I get married", I say the words out loud. Perry twitches like I would have punctured him with a sharp knife.

"I'm sorry if that's a problem to you – Too", I breath the words silently, because my voice is about to break.

"I'm sorry to ask but, Why?", Perry wonders. "It's just.. Because – "I try, but my voice cuts off. I turn around, so I wouldn't have to stand his impression that was creating millions of questions at once as soon as I opened my mouth. I was afraid he'd use everything I'd say against me.

"I want to give something of myself solely to one person – Something you can't create or mimic. Something that only I have.. And I want to wear that white veil someday with a pride.." I say silently as I try not to cry while making my confession.

Without saying a word Perry closes me into his arms.

"Those are great reasons", Perry consoles me after few minutes.

"You are not mad?" I ask.

"No", he mutters as he ponders, "I'm just overwhelmed – No one has ever said 'No' to me". I turn to look at him.

"That came out with a wrong tone", Perry laughs, " I mean.. There has never been a time that someone wouldn't want to have sex with me.. It's usually the opposite way – Wait that didn't come right either!" he tries out as he sits down. I watch him choosing carefully his words. He looks even more seductive like that; pondering everything so deeply that the words started to radiate from him.

"I'm not going to lie – I like sex", he starts, "And thanks to my parents good genes I have the looks that guarantee that I can have it pretty much whenever I want.. But you –", Perry talks as he turns to look at me. I sit down so I could meet his gaze.

"It's like you'd have a shield or something and I'm not sure weather or not I like it".

"It's not a shield.. It's simply a choice I made", I tell him.

I stare at Perry for few long minutes before speaking again.

"Is this too much for you?" I ask.

"No – I'm just thinking", he starts, "What does marriage mean to you then? Other than the self-claimed license to have sex". I can feel myself blush a bit by his words.

I take a better seat.

"It means that I have formed a deep special bond with the one I love the most. It means that I have legal right to take care of him and we have more opportunities to make our dreams come true", I explain. Perry seems surprised.

"What? Too main-stream?" I ask.

"I was one hundred percent sure that it means you want to settle down and assemble sweet little family and all", he admits.

For a second I feel a cold sting in me.

"No.. Even I want to wait until I have sex.. I have no intention to have kids.. Like ever – Don't get me wrong I love kids and all – !!" I confess.

"—You just don't want to have your owns", Perry continues. I nod in shame.

"My turn to make hard confessions", Perry says, "I can't have children of my own". I stare at him in confusion and shock. Part of my brain starts to ask if he was OK or not.

"I'm not sick or anything.. I got vasectomy"

"Can I ask why?" I blurt.

"Sure", he answers as he goes on , "I was sixteen when I turned into father. My girlfriend at the time didn't want to abort the baby, neither did she want to put him on adoption so she kept him"

"So you have a son?" I ask. Perry nods at me.

"Second time was a hook-up on a bar. I was too drunk to function like decent person so this one woman took advantage of my state and got herself pregnant.. Had the guts to try to make me pay allowance.. Her girlfriend however felt bad for me so they admitted to the court that I was nothing but a free sperm donor" he tells me.

Air seems to get lighter between us.

"That's when you decided you'd prevent yourself from having kids" I understand.

" – That and joining to AA" Perry whispers as he breaths in and out, "I had no idea I'd feel like this while talking about this", he admits in a shock.

"Like what?" I hurry myself.

"Insanely shocked and relieved". I can see a hint of a smile on his face.

"That's a hell of a lot to keep in", I remind him.

Perry pulls the collar of his shirt like he'd be suffocating in it.

"Are you OK?" I ask.

"No", Perry admits as we settle down to lay on the bed, "I mean I am.. But in a way I'm not".

"Do you wish me to leave or something?" I dare myself to ask.

"It did cross my mind – ", he admits as he turns to look at me.

"But?", I wonder. I couldn't speak after that at all. I had never had that deep conversation with anyone.

"I honestly don't know" Perry says as he stares at me, "But at the moment I don't even care. I really like spending time with you – Just like this".

"I've really liked this too", I tell him back.

"Can't we just keep going on with this weirdness for a minute longer and just – ?" Perry suggests. "That sounds good to me", I answer with a smile.

"I still want to admit that I would have wanted to make love to you", he tells me.

"If it is possible.. I want you to wait", I whisper.

I will wait

I get out of the bed while Perry was still
snoring. I decide to get us something to eat. I take the
key and head out to find some convenience store. As I
am heading back I stop by to look at a statue of some
woman. I was going to take a picture of it as a memoir
when I heard someone coughing.

"Got some light?" croaking male voice asks.
Before I have even answered I've been taken hold of
my arm. Naturally, I jerk back – away from the man
who's repeating his question.
"No, I don't smoke so I don't carry a lighter with me –
Sorry", I answer with the most polite way I could.
"Has anyone ever told you that you're pretty as fuck?",
man asks then while placing his cigarette on his lips. I
shook my head as an answer and try to move away.
"Pretty as fuck – Pitty fuck", man goes on as he
slumbers back to my way. I could sense the smell of
sweat and alcohol on him.
"I'm heading town you know.. Any chance you'd be
heading same way?" man bombards me.
"No, I'm not heading to town", I tell him silently.

"Oh c'mon.. I'll buy you something", man prompts me. I could barely think he'd carry enough money for the bus ride, even I reminded myself that looks could be just that much misleading.

"That won't be necessary", I declined.

"Am I not good enough for you?" man bolts then.

"No.. It's nothing like that – " I hurry myself as the man seems to transform into something. His eyes start to glow in rage and his hands are turning into fists.

"You pitty fucks are all the same! Always misleading poor guys like me with that smile and with those clothes – !!" man hisses. I back away from him for few steps more.

"Thanks for waiting me" sudden voice interrupts us. Perry takes me into his protective arms and ties me in. I can't help but to inhale his comforting fragrance and tie my hands around him to keep myself from shaking.

"Can I help you sir?" I can hear Perry ask from the man who flees the area without hesitation and I feel strong enough to ease my grip from Perry.

"Thank you", I thank him.

"Don't mention it – You were still waiting for me, right?" he belittles.

"Waiting for what?" I ask. My recent shock was blurring my thoughts.

"Are you still willing to wait for someone to be with you – **To accept your terms**?"

"I'm always waiting for that, it seems" I admit.

Perry takes hold of my hand as I try to leave. "Can you wait for me to be ready to do that?", he asks me then, "Can you wait for me to be able to ask you to be mine someday?" Perry asks with steady look on me.

"I can wait" I assure him as tears rise into my eyes.

"It will be sooner that our first date", he jokes.

"I will wait", I promise with a smile on my face.

Bunny

Echo

I'm about to fell when I can sense strong, intense grip on my waist.

"You'll get killed with those heels"

"I just slipped", I belittle as I turn around. There he stands – Man close to my age, maybe bit older with military cut hair. There was water pouring from his clothes and I can see he was not wearing any jacket.

"You're going to catch a fever like that", I point out.

"Don't worry about it", he laughs.

"Fair enough", I tell him back, "You may let go of me now".

"What if I wouldn't want to?" he asks back in a teasing voice as he looks down to his arms. I now notice that I was holding my hands on his. Something in him kept me captive. For a minute it felt like I could have just sunk into his moss green eyes.. And God knows I wanted to.

To break from his spell I place my hands to frame his face.

"Wanted or not Good-Looking, I still have to go". He laughs at that and lets go off me.

"Can I have your number – To ask you out some day?" he asks. When I can't say a word he asks for my name.

"Bunny", I tell him back.

"Aldo", he introduces himself, "I moved here recently".

"Bunny.. I've lived here for three years now".

"So.. How's with that number?", Aldo asks.

"You'll just have to wait", I tease him as I hurry myself to the bus.

In a buss I can't stop thinking about his grip on me. Then I laughed at myself for being so naive to be amazed by something like that. But through out the all day he kept on haunting in the back of my head.

. . .

When I got back home I was surprised to smell paint when I got to my floor. I turned to the way of the smell and saw that one corridor window was open along with one apartment door. Out of curiosity I peeked in and saw Aldo painting a wall.

He turned to look at me immediately.

"Bunny with her high heels", he greets me. His apartment echoed a bit.

"Aldo", I greet him, "So – Some DIY?".

"Yeah.. Landlord gave me a permission to get rid of the awful shade of violet and change it to something less.. Nerve-wracking", he explains as he pointed at a patch of hideously looking dark violet that reminded me of a brothel. Everything was in a lot lighter shade now.

"Impressive", I say out loud.

"Do you by any chance happen to have a paper and a pen?" he asks suddenly.

"Sure" I answer as I place my groceries to the doorway and take the asked items from my bag. As I try to handle them to him he shook his head with devious grin.

"Just give me your number", he tells me.

"Nice try", I admit as I toss the pen and paper to the grocery bag and hand him a bottle of beer.

"Not a bad consolation prize – Yet the number would be nicer", Aldo thanks me, "Any reason for not giving me that? I assume you have a phone?"

"Enjoy your beer Aldo", I advise him as I leave.

When I get inside of my own apartment I collapse to the hall.
I simply burst into tears.
How much I wanted to give him my number but couldn't.
Just couldn't.

Minutes passes and I slowly get up and make through my break down. As I'm placing the groceries to their rightful places Chastity comes home.

"I'm home!", her voice announces. When she comes to the kitchen she nearly falls down out of shock.

"What happened?" she demands as she takes holds of me – Wiping my face. Apparently some of my makeup needed some serious fixing up to do.

"I just got spooked", I belittle.

"With what?" "By the new neighbor.. He asked for my number", I tell her.

"Oh honey", she laughs while hugging me.

We both had the same anxiety when it came to men and phone numbers. I guess that was one of the 'dangers' of our profession.

"I bet he means well", Chastity assures me.

"Yeah.. He wanted to ask me out", I tell her.

"Shame on you Bunny", she scolds me, "I saw him and he's hot. What the heck is wrong with you?"

"I'm just an everyday-idiot", I say out loud.

"Stupid potato", we say at the same time. It was our inside joke which we both had long time ago forgot the origin of.

"Let's make something to eat – Before the damn phone rings", Chastity suggests with an irritated voice. I take her working phone and put the sounds off.

"Can't answer it if you don't hear it", I tell her.

"You are a genius".

"No, I'm the stupid potato".

Actress of Self-Hurting Play

I walk into a restaurant far fancy of the ones I've ever been, and there has been quite a lot of those places. I tiptoe with my high heels to the check-in-desk.

"Hello, is Mr. Bennet here yet?" I greet the man behind the desk.

"He is.. And you are?" he asks.

"His date, Ms. York", I introduce myself with an elegant smile.

"While yes – He's been expecting you", man tells me with a grand smile. I exhale on the inside. It was always hard to please restaurants 'front-guard' for they didn't want women like me indoors. Apparently I had the most perfect camouflage to blend in.

After leaving my coat I am directed to a remote table with a view over the city.

"Ms. York, pleasure to meet you". I study the man, on his late forties, early fifties with lovely big, brown and kind eyes and naturally graying hair. He was tall, but not too tall and his body physique told me that he kept himself in a good care. Not a bad customer on that department.

"It's nice to meet you too Mr. Bennet. I'm sorry that I am a bit late", I greet him back with a way that would have made even my late great-grandmother proud.

He helps me to sit down and takes a seat for himself too. I can see that he is nervous.

"I took a liberty to order us a drink Ms.. – ", he tells me when I interrupt him.

"Bunny", I tell him. He looks puzzled.

"My name is Bunny", I explain.

"Oh right.. ", he understands. He gets blushed.

"I'm Damien", he tells me then when waiter brings us champagne.

"What's the occasion?" I ask before touching my glass.

"Do we need one?" Damien wonders.

"No – I was just curious if there was any", I belittle.

"To be honest.. This is my first time with – ", he points at me with full hand gesture before continuing, "After my divorce.. I mean I have tried to ask out people but nothing really has worked out and I just didn't want to go the – ".

I take a gentle hold of his hand.

"It's all alright.", I calm him.

"No one will have a clue of the true nature of this setting. Your secret is safe", I whisper to him.

"To You", I salute him with my glass.

After the awkward dinner I go to get my coat while Damien goes to get his car. Apparently he didn't have a jacket at all, but then again; he had his own car. "Are you good at speaking to other people?" he asks as we sit to his car.

"I'd say that to be true", I answer.

"How about if they ask about me, how did we met and all that?" he wonders.

"I tell them that you asked me out and we went to have a lovely dinner where you were so shy that it melt my heart in a way that I wanted to meet you again", I say to him. Damien turns to look at me with a smile.

"You're good", he laughs. I shrug my shoulders and bat the back of his hand.

We get to the location of the big revealing party of something. Apparently Mr. Bennet was a big shot since we drove our car to the front where many people came to greet him. It was a party not big enough to catch the eye of the paparazzi's. This was more like own party of the working team. I took a firm grip on his left arm. I could sense that it made him feel good about himself.

"Who's she?" some woman asked as we entered in. She was on her early thirties and with her hair down she looked a bit friendly, but her face was sour.
"This is Bunny", Damien introduced me, "And this is Nina. Bunny – Nina, Nina – Bunny".
"Nice to meet you. So you work together.. Should I be jealous?" I tease Nina. I could read from Damien's reaction that I was gaining massive points with that.
"Oh no.. No.. Like you said. We just work together", Nina tries to laugh off her terror of my short observation. Damien takes me to the buffet.
"You are good", he whispers.
"So you and her.. You asked her out?" I ask.
"We did go on for couple of dates but then she said that she wasn't looking on anything *that* serious"

"Too bad for her then", I sigh as I give a light kiss on Damien's cheek for everyone to see.

"Is there any food I should avoid.. In case of an allergy?" I breath to his ear, as I would actually tease him with something *more* interesting.

"No", he answers as some man comes to us.

"Will!" Damien greets him.

Worth Every Dime

"What are you thinking at?" Damien's voice asks. I come back from my thoughts and turn to face him. For a second I wait him to disappear and everything to be a bad kind of dream but he remains there.

"I'm thinking about all this", I start weakly as I remember that I was supposed to act a role.

"Tell me more about your work", I demand him as I turn my back on him, not allowing Damien to lead my thoughts away of the matter. I sense him moving to lean on a pillow. Then he starts to speak.

"There's not much to tell.. I create the art and the landscapes with my team. It's really not that big of a job", he explains as he goes on.

"For now, there's just me, Nina and Will in the main team.. No one else, but we have tons of helping hands making the brilliant details", Damien continues.

"So.. Nina and Will are on the same line with you on the 'food-chain'?" I wonder.

"Yes and No", Damien admits, "If I weren't there they'd be clueless what to do since I'm the only one who has met the guy who wrote the script".

I decide that it was time for me to look at him again.

"Well.. Doesn't that make you the Boss of the team", I say clearly.

"I think you could say that", Damien admits as he closes me into his arms, "But I still think we're on the same line for – ", he tries to correct me but he gets lost with his words.

"Thank you Bunny.. These past few hours have been the best hours after nearly three years", he thanks me.

"You're welcome", I say back as I place my head on a pillow.

"So.. Do you always seduce your – ?" Damien tries to ask.

"I understand that you're curious.. But it's not a matter of which we should talk about", I tell him gently as I pull myself back to other side of the bed.

"I am sorry – I didn't mean to insult you", he apologizes.

"Like I said. I understand", I lie. I really didn't. What was it with men that they wanted to know stuff like that? I haven't talked about those matters even with my co-workers.

"I was just wondering about *your work*", Damien explains.
"Don't worry your mind with it", I say to him, "I don't do anything I wouldn't want to do". I can see that my words sooth him.

"What would you like to do next?" he wants to know.
"Can we order a pizza?" I ask without even thinking. I was starving. Damien looks at me bit stunned at first before a smile starts to radiate from his eyes to his lips. "Sure", he agrees.

Damien hands me a bathrobe while he puts on some clothes to himself.
"Feel free to use the bathroom – I wont join you", he tells me.
"What kind of pizza do you like?"

"Surprise me Damien", I tempt him. Even I'd normally go with vegetarian. But most men went crazy-mode when woman wanted pizza and then they'd say they wanted the vegetarian one.

I take my bag and head to the bathroom where I fresh myself up and switch the little black dress into a skirt and top. I did have a blouse to go with it, but Damien's apartment was so warm that I felt like I didn't need it. As I come out from the bathroom I find Damien in the living room.

"Do you play games Bunny?" he asks.

"Not that much" I admit.

"I figured we could pass time while waiting for the pizza.. It's vegetarian. I hope you don't mind" "Veggie-Man.. Wouldn't have thought of you.. Then again you did eat mushroom ravioli at the restaurant", I wonder. Damien smiles at me.

. . .

Pizza-delivery man was shocked to see a woman sitting on Damien's couch. I acted my best to make an impression that this was totally normal, something that he hadn't just figured out about Damien yet. That all those other times he had delivered the vegetarian pizza there would have been woman involved. The guy was stunned so much that he nearly forgot to get a payment.

"Poor guy", Damien stated as he placed the pizza box on the table.
"Just take one, no need to be that presentable", he tells me as he takes one slice himself. Yet, I take a napkin to avoid grease-stained fingers. Damien's impression tells me that he liked the way I disobeyed him a bit. I was just glad that I was able to fulfill his fantasy.

For my surprise I end up playing games with Damien 'till noon.
But like every other gig – I knew that I had to wrap it up.

"Thank you Bunny.. I've had a great time", Damien tells me as he stares at me in admiration.
"That is what I do", I tell him as he gives me an envelope full of greenbacks.
"This is too much", I hesitate.

"You were worth every dime", he tells me as he pinches my cheek playfully before kissing another one.

"Take care of yourself Damien", I tell him.

"You too Bunny", he tells me back.

I place the envelope to my bag and head outside to the street to take a cab.

I was exhausted.

I wanted to go home and take a shower.

Forget Damien and everything that related to him.

Just like after every time.

With everyone.

It's a Date!

I take a long route home to clear my head. For my own surprise I came home late, it was already tomorrow. I wonder where the time had gone. Just few seconds ago it had been noon and I had left Damien's apartment and now I was sneaking my way with my heels not to wake my neighbors at four in the morning.

As I'm at my door I'm surprised by Chastity who opens the door with a smile on her face,
"Come on in!" she's warm and kind as not usual. For my surprise Aldo comes behind her, waving his hand. I'm stunned as I step inside while Chastity closes the door behind me.
"It's alright Bunny, he came with good intentions", she calms me. I can feel myself relax a bit.
"So.. Have you been waiting here all night?" I start as we sit down in the living room, all of us across each other.

They surprise me with synchronized nods.
"Yes", he tells me.
"I'm sorry – ", I start.

"Oh, don't worry about it. Aldo knows you were at work", Chastity speaks. I look at Aldo and feel disgusted with myself – I can actually feel the pizza coming up my throat. But like any good girl out there I made a tired smile on my face and carried on with the show.

"Yeah.. I had long shift", I belittle.

Aldo looks at me like he'd sense something he couldn't quite figure out.

"Since you were so stubborn not to give your number for me to be able to ask you out I decided that I would wait for you to come home and *then* I would ask you out", Aldo explains.

"That's – That's very sweet of you", I start as I see Chastity mouthing at me:

"*Just go out with him! Can't you see he's HOT!*"

"Fine.. I'll go out with you for this once. Will you then stop stalking me?" I agree.

"No", Aldo laughs. "Just give me a sec – I fresh myself up a bit", I tell him.

"More coffee?" Chastity offers to him as I hurry myself to my bedroom and close to door.

"OK.. Way to go Bunny", I curse to myself as I check my makeup and change my skirt into jeans and heels into sneakers. That was about it. I went back to the living room.

"That was quick", Aldo admires.

"I could also go to sleep like normal people would do after they come from work", I remind him as he gets up. I take my coat and my handbag and share a look with Chastity as I leave my work phone on the table. I can see her putting the sounds off. I was officially off the clock.

Give it a Try

I close the door behind me as Aldo walks a bit ahead of me.

"So – Where are we heading?" I ask.

"To get some coffee, for a start", he answers with a smug smile.

"You know.. I would have given you my number.. Eventually" I tell him.

"I'm not that kind of a guy who likes to be on hold", Aldo admits.

"So.. Does that make you kind of a guy who always gets what he wants?" I wonder. He stops and turns to look at me.

"No", he answers as he takes hold of my waist, "I'm a guy who felt there was something more than what there was said out loud.. And I knew I'd go nuts if I wouldn't even try to obtain to it". Aldo keeps his gaze strongly on mine. I felt like I wanted to kiss him, but then again that would have been what he wanted and I wanted to punish him a bit for making me want to do something.

Then I realized that it wasn't what I was used to.
I was never the one to be seduced.

He lets me go with a snicker.

"If there'd be any snow I'd throw a ball on you", I admit.

"Well I better keep my guard on that then" Aldo laughs while opening a door to a coffee shop.

I take one strong coffee while he settles for one sad looking regular next to my huge 'on-the-go-cup'. We walk a while and settle down on to a park bench to watch the sunrise.

"I'm hardly ever awake during the sunrise" I sigh.

"Hardly ever?" Aldo repeats.

"I work during the nights, remember?" I remind him.

"What is it that you do then? You don't look like construction worker, and since you don't smell like booze, I hardly would believe you'd work in a disco.. I don't buy a nurse or a doctor either", Aldo wants to know.

I can feel my heart skipping a beat.

"It can't be that bad", he prompts me. "It is", I sigh.

"Are you an assassin?" he asks in a shock. I laugh at that.

"No – No!", I deny.

"I'm an escort", I tell him then. I watch his impression which remains the same, for my surprise.

"You know.. A call-girl?" I explain to him.

"OK", he settles. "O – K?", I ask back, stunned by his reaction.

"For a second I was afraid that you were an assassin, so an escort is *huge* improvement", Aldo explains as he takes a mouthful of his coffee.

"So.. What do you do for a living?", I ask.

"I am a construction worker", he reveals with a smile that radiates from his eyes.

I look at the view for a minute before saying anything.

"Look.. You can say it if you find it any – "

"Did I say anything about your work? No. I'm OK with it", Aldo interrupts me as he takes hold of my jawline with his warm fingertips, "It's what you do – Not who you are", he reminds me.

He kept me captive with his gaze for a long minute. Then all the sudden he gets up.

"Are you ready to go?" he asks.

"Ready to go where?" I ask back.

"Just.. Come along", he teases me. I place my empty coffee cup into a bin and fallow him up to the buss stop.

"Where are we going?"

"You'll see", he says.

"I'm having hard times with you", I say under my breath.

"You wish", he says back with even lower voice. I feel a good kind of chill going through my spine.

We get on to a buss and for my surprise he pays us both and gives me a window seat.

"Where is this buss going?" I ask.

"I don't know.. I've never taken this route", he answers.

"What?"

"Kidding!" Aldo reassures me.

"So is this stuff what you normally do on your day off?" I wonder as I try to trace the city map in my head. Aldo just gives me a smile.

"You really aren't going to tell me anything?" I ask. His smile only gets wider.

"Fine – Let's play it your way then"

"This isn't a game", he tells me, "But if it were.. I'd be loosing it", he tells me as he pushes the stop button.

No Reality

I gaze the building in front of my eyes. It was an old movie theater.

"You shouldn't take a girl to movies on your first date", I tease him.

"I don't care about the rules", Aldo tells me as we get in. I was surprised that it was open on that early hours. "It's open 24/7", that's how they manage to survive in this place", Aldo explains, as he guesses my question.

We go to see some awful monster-movie which we laugh about so hard that if there would have been anyone else watching it we would have been thrown out.. But there weren't. There was just us.

"I'm starving.. What would you like to eat?" Aldo asks as we get out of the theater into a busy street. While we had been on our weird bubble inside someone had set the world alive once again.

"Anything is good for me"

"Breakfast it is then", Aldo decides as he takes hold of my hand and hurries us to the other side of the street to take another buss.

It starts snowing.

"I can finally make that snowball", I tease him.

Laughter escapes from Aldo's lips.

"What makes you so sure I won't throw one first?"

"Because you are a gentleman?" I try. I'm surprised to notice that we were heading back home.

As we get out of the buss I take some snow into my hands and pretend to make a snowball. Aldo holds his hands up.

"OK, OK! Please no snowballs! If you throw it there will be *no* breakfast!", he laughs. I clear my hand out of snow only to be given a snow wash on my face.

"Oh no you didn't – !" I curse as I take some snow and within seconds I throw snowballs at him.

"OK, OK, stop!" he laughs. I wont stop until he takes hold of me and forces us to go down to the snow.

"I said stop", he reminds me.

"Your eyes said different", I defend myself. He looks at me a minute before he gets up and lends me a hand.

"I guess it's no breakfast for me then", I say quietly.

"Maybe I let this one slide this time", he says as he takes hold of my hand and we walk to our building, but instead of leading me to my door we walk to his. "Breakfast", he ensures me. I nod at him.

Aldo's apartment was clean and very much like him, playful. He had managed to bring some basic furniture to there already. I guess being a man had it's perks; you'd always have hands to help you out to lift heavy stuff. For a woman most of us depended on others to do so, for we weren't that strong by nature, we were expected to be fragile and weak. That's why most of us had such an incredibly strong minds, I guess.

I place my wet outdoor clothes to dry. After that I fallow him to the kitchen – living room area.
"So, what would you like to have?"
"Toast.. Eggs?" I suggest.
"Eggcellent choice", he jokes.
"Mind if I put some bell pepper with the eggs?"
"Fine by me", I tell him as I take the bread and place them into a toaster.
"Juice?" he offers.
"Yes please", I answer.

. . .

"Thank you for persuading me on to this date. I had fun time", I thank Aldo as I drink my glass empty. Aldo kept his gaze on me as he placed his plate on the table. Subconsciously, I mimicked him with my plate. "Was I correct with my observations? About the non-said things?" he wants to know. Without uttering another word I kissed him. This cat-and-mouse game was going to end on him winning it. Aldo kissed me back and didn't even try to take my clothes off.

All the sudden I was crying.

I place my head on his chest without saying a word.
"Did I do something wrong?", Aldo demands.
"No, nothing like that", I start quietly. I can sense him relax a bit.
"Just.. Too much", I analyze.
"Sorry", he laughs back as he pets my hair. Tiredly I look at him as he looks back at me without saying a word..

Few hours later I find myself still in his arms. Slowly I free myself from his protecting hands and sneak my way to the hall to put on my shoes. Rest of my stuff I figure I could be able to carry on my hands.

As I try to open the door Aldo blocks me between his arms on a doorway.

"Are you leaving without even saying anything – That's just cold. Can't you at least tell me your number or where we stand at the moment?" he asks in disbelief. Then Aldo lowers his arms back down, waiting for me to response to him. I'm speechless.

"Bunny?" he asks.

"I can't –", I tell him back in stutter. For a minute we just stare at each other, standing still without a clue how to move on.

Then I make my choice and I try to get my belongings from the floor (which I had dropped there out of shock). For my surprise he embraces me with a long lasting kiss.

"I just can't do it – And I wouldn't want to say no to you", I admit. I look at his eyes. I meant what I had just said. I wanted to say yes but my common sense was telling me to stop. Aldo deserved someone better than me.

”Then don't”.

I stare at his eyes with question.
”I wouldn't care any less if you are an escort or not” Aldo explains to me. My head starts to spin and I take hold of the wall to stay foot.
”I date and sometimes sleep with other people” I hear myself telling him.
”Could be worse – At least you're not killing them”, Aldo assures me, ”I accept that not every relationship is like in a fairy-tale”.
”That sounds charitable now.. But wait for few months and you'll hate me”, I say back.
”I wont hate you”, he assures me, ”Can't you not give me a try?”
”Aren't you listening a word I say? – ” I try to put together the mental image but I can't.
”I am – Don't get me wrong”, Aldo interrupts me, ”Please – Give us a try”.

For a minute I'm only able to stare at nothing as I try to remain calm and understand what I've just heard.

"You are too good for me" I manage to say.

"I am not", Aldo tells me as he comes closer to me. I allow him to touch me again as he helps me to gain back my sense of gravity.

"I like about you a lot Bunny.. But I'm not going to ask you to do something that frightens you this much", he admits quietly.

"Why not?" I demand, "You've been convincing me over for the past few days and you give up on me now? What makes you think I'm not worth of trying something that scares me from the beginning?". He's in shock of my statement. That's when Aldo closes me back to his arms from the judgmental world.

"I need to get back home", I try. My own voice betrayed me. I didn't want to go home.

"Then leave", he teases me.

"Stop it.. I need to sleep"

"You can sleep here", Aldo reminds me.

"Just sleep?" I ensure of him.

"Yes", he agrees.

Moment of Clarity

When I get back home it's late. Chastity had gone to work, according to a message on the fridge. I close the curtains and put on some dim lightning on. I never cared to put on all of them. After that I head to take a shower before settling down to my bedroom. I put some music on and head to the fridge to make myself a bowl of cereals. I was happy at that moment. Tired, but happy.

After checking the news I wash my teeth and head to the living room.
"Hi there" Chastity greets from the door. She had just came from her gig.
"How was your date?"
"Great", I tell her back as I rose to sit.
"Just great?"
"Yeah", I belittle.

"What shall we talk about then since you are that mysterious?" she wonders.
"Oh, how was work?" I nearly throw up. Good for me she was in the hall and didn't see it. For almost two

days I haven't even thought of my work and then – She had to break the spell.

"Fine", I tell her as I get up.

"What?" Chastity asks.

"Nothing – Sometimes you are just mean", I tell her while I go to my room and close the door.

. . .

Weeks went by and me and Aldo were hitting of quite well. More and more I spent time with him, the more and more I started to pick my customers based on the escort-theme. I wanted to be more like fine jewelry for them rather than a playing doll.

Then our fridge decided to broke down..
And we needed some money with Chastity to replace it.

So there I was at one of my most demanding customer for I knew he would be able to hand me half of the money for the fridge by one night.

. . .

I barely get indoors when he is already on to me like a hungry beast. I try to act pleasingly to him when something suddenly hits me. I didn't want to be there. I wanted to go away – No fridge on the whole wide world was worthy of this. I wanted to leave so bad that I started to panic.

"No", I say strongly, "I need to go". I free myself from Zachary's hands and grab my bag with an ease. I haven't had wanted to mislead him at any point but I had to leave from there immediately.

"What do you think you're doing?" he taunts me.

"I am leaving", I inform him.

"Hell you're not! What the fuck is this?" he curses as he takes hold of me.

"Let me go", I command as he tries to force me to come along with him. I hit Zachary's lungs empty with a well-practiced punch by using my elbow and manage to free myself some time to get out of the bedroom. But he doesn't stop his pursue over me.

"Just leave it Zach", I warn him as he commands me to submit. Zachary takes hold of me again, this time by pushing me on to a wall; pinning me into it by using all of his over six foot tall body to do so.

I can't even recognize his words over the sound of my terrified heartbeats. As he pulls me closer to kiss me I bite his lip so hard that he starts to bleed. First he tries to ignore it for he's trying to pull down my jeans, but the pain and the sense of falling blood gets to him. "You bitch!" he curses as he tries to hit me, but I am quicker and he manages to hit his hand on the wall. I kick him to his groins and manage to get some space between us.

"Well that was just stupid", Zachary says in furious tone as he wipes his face clean from blood.
"I said 'No'", I tell him back.
"I have no obligations to have sex with you", I remind him. Zachary looks around him and I can feel his rage starting to radiate.
"Just call for another girl.. That's all there is to it", I try.

That's when he bolts and launches himself at me. With an ease he pins me again on the wall. I use all my body strength to try to get past him with no use.

Zachary hits me on the face before trying to pull my legs apart.

"No!" I cry.

"You know how this works! I call – You deliver!" he hisses.

"Just stop!" I command, "Do you wish to be arrested and be put down in jail?!"". That's what hits Zach like a bat. He stares at me in horror. He lets go off me and backs off.

Zachary walks past the room and hands me my bag.

"Go", he commands. Without even hesitating I take my bag and run off. After few moments outside I start to hiccup in the means of trying to cry but I force myself not to. Zachary wasn't worth of my tears.

When I get to my apartment door I can hear Aldo's door opening.

"I thought I heard your heels", he greets me. I can hear him walking in my way. I turn to look at him and his impression shifts.

"What happened?!" he asks in a shock.

"Bad gig?", I suggest as I open my door. I leave the door open for him to fallow. I can hear him running to close his own door before coming back. I'm already taking off my heels when he closes the door. I can sense him being agitated.

"Leave it Aldo", I tell him as I go to kitchen to get some cold water.

He fallows me there and leans to the counter before talking.

"I've said earlier that what you do doesn't bother me – But you seriously can't expect that it wouldn't bother me if someone beats you up", Aldo tells me before he takes me to his arms. That's when I start to cry.

"Jesus", he breaths as he examines me, "Is that your blood?"

"Not all of it", I admit.

"What happened?" he demands to know. I shook my head as an answer.

"I can't help you if you don't talk to me", Aldo reasons me.

"You already *did* help me", I say slowly as I lean back to face him, "I don't want to do this anymore", I inform him as I point down myself, to my clothing, to my broken makeup, hair – All to the visual effects to lure men towards me like a moth into a flame. Aldo nods slowly as he realizes what I was saying. I sit on the counter and he joins me.

"Do I need to beat him up for you?"

"I did pretty good job myself", I tell him with sad laughter.

Without saying anything else Aldo closes me to his arms and just holds me.

Lucid Dream

I wake up the next morning when Aldo kisses me on the cheek. He had refused to leave me alone for the night and since Chastity didn't come home early Aldo had stayed. I felt happy that he did – It made me feel better.

"See you later", he whispers to my ear. I nod at him as an agreement. Then he leaves.

For a minute I'm tempted to stay in bed but I knew myself better.
So I get up and head to the shower before heading out of the apartment.

I wasn't going to stop myself now.

For a minute I wonder the line of order for my actions but after seeing my face in the elevator mirror I knew that I should see someone from the medical team first. My steps become miraculously silent as I step in to the medical center. I take the question form from the nurse behind the desk who stares at me in shock. I just thank her.

Within few minutes I was face to face with a doctor-woman who read my papers like she'd be reading a horror novel.

"So – You came here to?" she stuttered.

"I was wondering if you could back me up.. I want to study myself into a proper profession.. I want to be able to keep on the track of time.. I want – ", I sob, "I want to become normal". Doctor bursts into tears before me.

"I'm sure I can do that.. Anything you want sweetie".

I wondered how long I had waited for this to happen.
The direction of my life to change.

And all I had been asked to do for myself was..
To ask for Help.

I was given an appointment to see psychiatric nurse on the fallowing week who would determine if/when I needed some more help. I was happy for my progress. Next thing I did was quitting in the escort company. That was slightly harder than going to see a doctor for they really didn't like to let people go – They tried to talk you over. They even had the guts to tell me that I'd be begging my job back before the end of the month.

I said nothing back.
I just simply left my memory-cleaned phone on the table and left.

Silence & Wind chime

Fairies and one misbehaving Dodo

I look at what I have with a smile on my face.
Delilah stands next to the window with our close to
four-year-old girl on her arms. They're looking out
without noticing me standing on the doorway. I can
read Delilah's lips as she talks about fairies that are too
scared to come over to dance on the morning light –
Even it was their music that was playing outside.

Then Delilah looks at her wind chime; my
wedding present for her from the day that we said 'I do'
for each other and she turns to look at me – I guess I
still haven't learned how to walk more silent or she has
sixth sense or something.

"*Daddy – Fairy music!!*" Rose signs to me with
a smile on her face, "*Listen!*" she commands. I feel like

my daughter would have just shot me on the very heart of mine.

"Rose.. Daddy can't hear them.. But he can *see* the fairies whenever he likes", Delilah explains to her.

"I want to see them too", Rose mumbles.

"She didn't mean it", Delilah apologizes.

"I know", I tell her back as I come to watch the wind chime.

I can see it's movement, but I don't hear it – I have never heard it. I am deaf. I can recognize very, *very* loud sounds, but I can't tell you what they are. I'm what doctors like to call 'profoundly-deaf'. My mom is profoundly deaf, my father is hearing disabled, I have three siblings; two sisters, other one deaf like me, other one hearing and a brother who has a hearing disability – yet he can hear pretty well with his hearing aids. Delilah and Rose are both hearing persons.. And I'm more than happy to have them both in my life.

"Who wants to have breakfast?" I ask as I turn to look at the two of the most beautiful women in my life.

"*Me*", they sign at the same time.

"Well good.. I am hungry too" I joke as Delilah puts Rose on the floor.

"I feed Dodo", she announces. **Dodo** is our dog. I have no idea how Rose molded 'Tonto' into 'Dodo', yet that is the name dog is listening now.

"*Morning*", Delilah signs at me as she gives me a light kiss.

"*Morning.. Have you been up for long?*" I ask.

"*No*", she tells me back as we start to walk our way to the kitchen where Dodo is getting his breakfast.

"*Rose wanted to come to see you already, for she claimed to hear you use the bathroom*", I explained to my wife.

"*Well Rose was right.. I was up already*", Delilah admits.

"*I was scared that she'd trick me again*", I sigh.

"*She doesn't always trick you*", she laughs back.

"*But she can do it pretty easily to me*", I defend my point as I get bowl for Rose's oatmeal. I feel Delilah's laughter against my shoulder – The breath becomes different.

"Eat your breakfast, you trickster", I say to the little meanie as I place her to sit on her chair.

"*I don't trick you*", Delilah translates Rose's words for me.

"Alright.. I take your word from it.. But I'll make Dodo keep an eye on you", I tease her.

As I turn I see Dodo eating my breakfast.

"Bad dog!" I correct him, but the dog simply licks the plate clean, "I told you we should get a small dog", I tell to Delilah.

"Dodo makes me feel safe when you're not here", Delilah defends her four legged 'monster'.

"He eats from my plate!" I say back, showing my plate.

"Dodo.. You're a bad dog", Delilah talks to the dog. I can't help but laugh.

"I guess the fault is mine", I admit. Having a big dog means they have greater appetite.. And even Rose did feed him just a second a go.. He can still be hungry.

"*I'll make you something*", Delilah comforts me.

"*It's all good.. I take the rest of the oatmeal*", I tell her back as I take myself another bowl.

"Dodo is a bad, bad dog", Rose repeats.

"Yes he is.. But Daddy forgives him", I say to her. I don't want her to call Dodo 'a bad dog' all day long.

"*Why?*" she asks.

"Because that is what you do.. Look at him" I explain to her as I turn to look at Dodo with her. He's on the floor with paws on his muzzle – Ashamed.

"He is sorry", I tell to Rose. My daughter looks puzzled.

"If I do this", she says as she places her hands on her nose, "Does it mean Rose is sorry?". I laugh, Delilah laughs.

"No.. It's a dog sign", I assure her.

"Dogs can sign too?!" Rose asks in disbelief.

This little girl with her constant realizations of the world are just..

Priceless.

Week of Misfortune

"We'll be ready in a sec", Delilah tells me as she and Rose head to the bathroom. I take out my phone and start to check up my mail. My mom has sent me my weekly horoscope. She is an astrologer, so I just had to deal with her nonsense.

Your horoscope for the start of this week Matt:

This week is mostly full of misfortune for you. The stars aren't just agreeing with you at all. Don't try to do anything from the priority list of yours for it will not turn out well.

Love, Mom

Thanks mom, but I still got work to do. I work really hard – Even I'm deaf I have never let it affect on my work. I have my own business with my friend Jasper. We fix computers for small companies. I love what I do and so does Jasper. I do most of the actual working part when Jasper works as a face to our company. We also have our own 'interpreter' along with us, even Jasper does know how to sign and all we just figured that with a third person who tags along with me we can get more work done and so far that has worked like a dream.

My personal assistant, the interpreter is forty-five year old Martha. She is awesome. Her facial impressions (and her tone, I've heard) match with my way of impressing of myself with such accuracy that even Delilah admits that Martha seems to be able to read my very mind.

"Are you ready?", Delilah asks as I'm still holding my phone.
"Mom told me that this week will be full of misfortune for me", I tell her.
"For me she forcasted worries too – Is she alright?", she admits.
"I guess I should ask", I sign back. Was something bothering my mom? Was that the reason for the 'not-so-great' readings.
"Sorry.. I made you worry", Delilah apologizes.
"It's OK.. I'll go and meet her before work", I calm her. I get up and embrace her.

"I don't believe in horoscopes", I remind her.

After leaving Rose to her daycare and Delilah to her work I drive to my parents house. I walk to the door and press the bell. My mom comes to open it.

"Matt? – Why are you here? Aren't you supposed to go to work?" she greets me as we get in.

"Coffee?", she offers.

"Yes.. I'm here because you sent those more or less disturbing readings to me and Delilah.. Is something wrong?" I ask.

In 'Deaf World' being straight about your mind is OK. More than that.. It's pretty much the only way there is in communication.

"I'm fine! I'm fine!", mom promises, *"I was just telling you what I – "*

"Mom.. Please. Next time tell it differently", I beg her.

"I'm sorry that I worried you", mom signs to me while handing me some coffee.

"You should! You worried us both, me and Delilah", I tell her.

I see my dad coming to the kitchen.

"*Matt?*", he signs in wonder.

"*Hi dad!*", I sign him back – Letting my mom know that he is in the room too.

"*Good morning!*" mom greets him.

"*Why is Matt here this early?*" my dad keeps asking.

"*I gave him and Delilah their weekly reading and they got upset – Nothing more*", mom explains. I take my phone from my pocket and hand it to my dad so he can read what mom sent to me.

"*This needs to stop*", my dad signs to my mom while pointing at my phone before giving it back.

"*I just told what I –* ", mom starts but stops herself in the middle of the sentence, "*I was trying to be nice by warning you, that's all*".

"*Like I said.. Do it differently*", I tell her, "*Thanks for the coffee. I got to go to work now*".

Working with lunatics

"*Well good morning Matt, for nice of you to join us!*" Jasper, my friend since the third grade greets me as I enter into our office.

"*I know I'm late – About ten minutes – Spare me from the lecture*", I greet him back. Then I look at Martha. She's wearing a 'joker-hat'; the one you'd see on playing cards.

"*What?*" I ask.

"*Too much? I thought this would be something fun, for the third place is a game arcade*", Martha wonders.

"*You're not wearing that hat*" I sign to her with disgust for the ugly hat.

"*I told her that you wouldn't like it*", Jasper reveals.

"*I like it*", Martha signs from the distance.

"*Well you can keep it – When I don't see it*" I tell her.

Then all the sudden she and Jasper start to make weird movements and their mouths move with similar movements. Then they start to laugh. I realize that the radio is on and they are singing and dancing. For me it looks like someone would have released a doze of nerve gas and they'd be having a seizure.

"*That looks so stupid without a sound*", I point out.
"*Matt.. It looks stupid **with** the sound too*", Jasper comforts me.

"*Are you ready Martha?*" I ask as I see her leaning at her work desk.
"*Born ready*", she answers before picking up her purse; that's all she needs. I go to pick up my gear that includes a backpack and a traveling bag with wheels. I'm prepared for nearly anything.
"*Have **fun***", I tease Jasper before going. I know he has tons of papers to do today.

"*Why were you late?*" Martha dares herself to ask as we get into the car.
"*Family things that turned out to be nothing*", I explain.
"*OK*", she settles.
"*How was your weekend?*", I ask politely.
"*It was fine.. Ben was bit feverish, but it was over this morning so he decided to go to school.. I'm nesting my phone like a chicken in case the fever gets back*", she tells me.
"*Sorry to hear that*", I sign to her before concentrating myself on driving.

The first place we go is some of our oldest clients. A coffee shop that offered free Wi-Fi to their customers. There was something wrong with the connection and their operator claimed that it was due the wrong equipment's. I guess the operator had sold them connection that wasn't suitable for the equipment's I had wired to the place a while ago. Why people didn't read my notes after I left? I had written all the numbers for them in order to avoid this situation.

"Matt!" Peter greets me. He knows how this thing goes, he talks to me and I either read his lips or stare at Martha while she interpreted. Martha doesn't exist to him at all – Unless I decide to sign and Martha starts to interpret me with speech.
"So good to see you, people are getting anxious", Peter talks, "I'm counting on you".
"Please don't.. Too much pressure", I joke at him.
"Coffee?" he asks as he *tries* to sign it.
"Wrong again", I tell him, "But coffee would be great".
"I have some tea with a scone, thank you", Martha orders.

While Peter goes to make our order I go straight to my signed post to figure out what was wrong. Without even thinking about coffee anymore I just start to work on it; Getting in the zone completely.

"It should be working now", I say out loud. I see Martha checking on her phone. She gives me thumbs up while biting her scone.
"What was wrong with it?" Peter demands to know.
"I can't explain it to you in English", I tell him truthfully. I get my cup of coffee. I watch Martha sign to me "*Thanks again you freaky wizard of Nerd-Land*".
"You're welcome", I say back.

Martha is looking at her phone. Her normal impression transforms into something different – Something was up.
"*What's wrong?*" I ask.
"*It's Ben.. He's feeling sick again*", Martha answers.
"*Go*", I tell her.
"*Are you sure? You have three other places –* " Martha speed-signs.
"*Martha.. Your son is sick*", I reason her.

"Thanks Matt.." Martha thanks me before we end our first meeting of today with Peter.

I drive Martha to pick-up Ben from school. Then I drive them to our office where Martha and Ben goes to their car. Jasper comes out of our office with confused impression.

"Ben got sick", I explain to him.

"How about rest of the – ?" Jasper wonders.

"They are all old customers.. They know me", I settle him as I watch my phone,

"Plus other one just canceled it seems".

"You lucky – " Jasper tells me without finishing his sentence.

"I know", I say to him as I get back to my car.

Just when my mom told me that stars wouldn't agree with me this week.

Better Time

Rest of the day goes by with an old routine. I'm more than happy to get Rose from the daycare and Delilah from her work – Just to drive home and spend time with them. Am I weird to admit that I like that all so much? I don't think so. Mondays were pretty much the only days we were able to spend time together this much. Plus; Rose isn't going to be a little girl forever; One day she'll turn out to be a teen who will hate her parents to her guts and right after shouting that to us she'll cry her eyeballs out claiming that we don't love her. Yet, I would tell her that as her dad I'd never stop loving her and neither would her mom, I'm sure.

So we needed to make good memories to remember..
Well, at least *I* needed good memories to remember when that time would come.

I watch Delilah come from Rose's bedroom while Dodo goes to his sleeping place.
"*Story of Golden Rose*", Delilah tells me with a sigh. It was their favorite story. She sits down to our kitchen

counter. I hug her tightly before I start to massage her neck; something I do every know and then for her.

"Why you have to work with computers, when you're so good at this?" Delilah asks when she turns around.

"Would you want me to give that much joy to other women and men out there?" I tease her. Delilah laughs at me. I lock her between the counter and me.

"I see", she says.

"What?" I ask.

"It's not good time for that now – I just got Rose to bed and – " Delilah worries.

"There will be better times to do **that**, but now this is all I want", I point out before I kiss her.

I can feel us being stared at.
I turn around and see Rose.

It's hard to be a parent;
Sometimes you just found yourself staying up to late hours..
Just because you were trying to convince your kid that monsters weren't having a tea party under the bed.

See Beauty

I'm driving Rose to her daycare and Delilah to work when I get a text from Martha. She's not coming to work today for she has gotten sick too. Seriously bad news. I was signed for two customer visits today and now I have to figure out a way to get myself another interpreter – And fast.

As I walk to our office Jasper shows me his phone. He has gotten the same message than I just did. *"Hi Matt"*, Jasper greets me.
"Hi Jasper.. What are we going to do?" I ask back.
"Is there any chance that Vanessa would be available?" Jasper asks hopefully.
"No", I tell him. Vanessa is my younger sister, the one who hears. Jasper hits his hand on the wall out of frustration.

"Should you just call them and tell them about our situation?" I ask nicely. I know that Jasper doesn't like to call for me, that is why we have Martha.
"I try", he answers. I get my gear bag and wait for him to make the call.

Jasper holds the phone in the way that I can't read his lips. It's annoying. They are talking about me, I know that, yet I have no idea **what** they are talking about me and yet I stand in front of Jasper. So I wait.

"Martha had called them. They're well aware of the situation and two of them are OK for you to go there by yourself.. Question is: Are you OK to go there by yourself?" Jasper explains to me. He has his phone on the table as he signs to me.
"I'm good.." I tell him back.
"Yes he's OK with it.. He'll be coming there right away", Jasper speaks, *"They'll be waiting"*, he signs while finishing the call.
"I'll call the other places at some point – I try to win them over", Jasper announces.

"Fine by me. Text me how it goes.. I'll try to ask how long is Martha going to be on sick leave.. And I guess if it's for long period of time I need to figure out someone to substitute her", I think.
"Sounds like a plan. See you at lunch", Jasper agrees with me. I go on my way to my first gig of the day.

The day turns out to be short, for not everyone wants to work with a man who doesn't hear. People are also extremely rude to us. Even we don't speak it doesn't mean we can't '*listen*'. Either way; I help Jasper with the paper work and head my tour to pick Rose up to her dancing class which was just around the corner from Delilah's work-place.

"Daddy – I don't think I want to be a dancer anymore", Rose surprises me while I was getting her out of the car.
"Why not?" I ask.
"Because you can't hear", she mutters. I close her in a gentle hug before I look at her again.
"Even I can't hear the music it doesn't mean that I wont see the beauty of your dance", I tell her. She smiles at me.
"Now let's go", I hurry her as we race to the door.

I sit in the lobby unlike majority of the parents who preferred to sit in the practice room. Delilah and I had decided along with few other parents to give our kids the right to practice on their own, making mistakes and trying again without we knowing every detail of it. They were able to astonish us when they'd show their performance. That's what I wanted Rose to be able to do. That's what Delilah wanted her daughter to do.

Orange Elephants and Happiness out of Small Things

Next day I got home Delilah has already picked up Rose – She got a lift from her co-worker after she explained that I was running late with my working schedule. I make a mental note for myself to thank the co-worker for helping us out.

As I drive my car to our drive way I'm surprised to see my mother-in-law's car in there. I didn't know she was coming to visit today.

I'm welcomed back home by Rose and Dodo while Delilah and her mother are in the kitchen.
"Daddy I learned how to draw an elephant today!" Rose tells me.
"You did?" I ask, "Can you show it to me?"
"Yeah", she says as she goes to get her drawing. I walk to the kitchen.
"Hi Matt!" my mother-in-law, Jo says to me. She doesn't know any sign language.
"Hi Jo" I greet back as Delilah waves her hand to me.

Rose hands me her drawing with a blue elephant on it. It's really cute.

"Do you like it?" she asks.

"*I love it*" I tell her. Rose smiles at me and goes to continue her doings.

"*She said that she'll make one for you.. What color you'd like her to use?*" Delilah interpreted for me.

"Make me an orange elephant", I tell to Rose. Orange was the one she didn't use that much.

"*OK*", Delilah signs for me from Rose. Jo smiles at us. I know that Delilah is speaking at the same time as she speaks so Jo would stay on the same page – I sometimes forget to do so.

"I go walk the dog", I tell them as I take the leash. Delilah nods at me as she continues her talk with her mother. Dodo runs to me with enthusiastic impression. This dog loves his walks. Rose looks at us but goes back to her art work. Apparently she doesn't want to come with us today. I look outside and see it had started to rain – No wonder Rose isn't feeling the urge to join us. She hates to wear her rain-gear.

"I go now", I say from the door.

Dodo is good dog on his blessed overtime with us. Originally he was Delilah's dog – Before he became **our** dog – They had been together since Dodo was a puppy, for Dodo's 'mom' was Jo's Great Dane, who had an accident with their neighbor's St. Bernard – And that is how three mix puppies were born. Even Dodo is a big dog.. It's the kindest animal you can find. When Rose was born he started to sleep in the nursery and whenever Rose started to cry he'd come to me or to Delilah to inform it. He'd take a hold of our clothes and pull, Delilah told me that he even *whined* a bit. I'm not sure what *whining* is, but I guess it's an annoying type of sound (Even I could hear in my past, I couldn't hear in **perfect** way – I was able to tell that people were speaking, emergency car was near, school bells were ringing and stuff like that).

I look at the dog who's walking nicely on it's leash. Some other people walk pass me with their dogs – Most of them nearly running. I can't understand them; It's just a rain – Buy yourself pair of rain boots and a raincoat.. Or an umbrella. Dodo looks at me and makes a face that reminds me of a smile. Then it wags it's tail.

He's happy. I'd like to be a dog sometimes; They know how to be happy out of the smallest things there are. At the moment the dog is happy for being walked outside.. In the rain, but still.

When I come back home I see that Jo's car is gone. I dry up Dodo carefully before allowing him to go to the rest of the house. Rose is playing in the living room. She has placed her drawing of the orange elephant on the kitchen table. Lights blicker; I turn and see Delilah.

"You're soaked", she states to me with disgust.

"I know", I tell her back. Still, she comes to hug me.

"Go change, I don't want you to get cold or anything", she commands me.

"OK.. But I'd like to know why Jo was here?" I ask.

"She brought Dodo's diet food", Delilah explains. Dodo is sensitive dog; he can't handle grains – Just like Delilah.

"I was afraid something had happened", I tell her.

"No.. I just told her earlier that you're late at work so she offered to bring the food by herself and she wanted to spend some time with Rose as well", she laughs
"Alright – That makes so much more sense", I sign to her as I head to change my clothes.

"Phone", Rose tells me as I'm building a 'Princess tower' to her out of plastic bricks.
"Phone or the computer phone?" I ask. Rose points at our computer where I see the video call symbol. I go to answer to it. It's Jasper.

"Hi", I greet him.
"Hi Matt!" he greets me back, *"I'm sorry to disturb you like this but I wanted to inform you that Martha's sick-leave is going to last longer than she announced"*, he tells me.
"No!!" I sign back. I'm disappointed, *"Why?"* I demand to know. Rose climbs her way to my arms as I sit next to the computer.
"Hi Rose!" Jasper talks to her.
"Her both sons are now sick. They have a stomach flue.. She thought it would be best for her to take at

least one whole week off so we wouldn't get sick too",
Jasper explains to me.

"*This will be a hard week*", I think.

"*I know*", Jasper agrees. I end the call.

"*Is something wrong?*" Delilah asks from me as
I turn around.

"*Martha's sons are sick and she's unable to come to
work. It's stomach flue*" I tell her.

"*Bad news*", she knows. I turn to look at Rose.

"I think we were at the middle of something.. But my
nose tells me that food is ready".

Words about living in Silence

There isn't just one way of being deaf. Just about anyone who has problems with hearing and engages the deaf culture can call themselves deaf – It doesn't mean that you need to be completely unable to hear; For example I have always told people that I'm deaf, even when I was able to hear something.

The most common assumption people make about deaf people is that we would have a super-vision or something. I'm telling you; we do not have a super-vision. Our eyes are just taking in more visual data in order to compensate the fact that there's so much information that we're not able to have. We do get distracted with visual things as much as you are distracted with noises; While trying to focus on conversation some sudden reflection of light is as much irritating to me as a loud sound is to you.

My ability to smell things is great and my skin is pretty sensitive to touch. I always wake up whenever Delilah taps me while I sleep. We have created 'tap-language'. Two taps and a hold means that Rose wants something. Three taps and a hold means that Dodo is in the need of attention. Then there's the least used one that contains three fast taps, two holds, and three fast taps again; Something is seriously wrong.. In case you didn't get it; Last one is the basic Morse code for **'S.O.S'**.

It has been hard for me and Delilah to make Rose understand that I can't hear. She gets frustrated at me sometimes when I have hard times to figure out what she wants. I wish there was a way for me to make her feel better, to be able to be the person she wishes me to be.. But I can only be me and try my very best.

Whenever we go out some place as a family I can read people's lips – Some people think that Rose is deaf too but she has been implanted because her mother is a hearing person. No – Rose is a hearing person. For the record; Me and Delilah are personally against implants. Delilah can't stand the idea of cutting the skull of a child. The thought makes me sick too to be honest. It's just *one* sense. You still have few others to use – Being deaf isn't the End of the World.

And that was what *hearing* people talk about my daughter and our family. Deaf people are trying to make me and Delilah to use sign language with Rose full 24/7; '*It's good for her for she will learn to impress herself strongly and –* ' No.. Just because I'm deaf it doesn't mean that the whole family is 'doomed' to live without enjoying sounds of human voices. Let me and Delilah do this the way that is good for us, alright? We use both, signs and voice – Equally. Yet when Delilah and I talk to each other we prefer to use sign language.

As a side note;

Please.
Stop talking about my family like that.

Our life – Our choices.
Thank you.

Hands

"Can you – With – For we – " woman talks to me as she reads her note in the way that I can't read her lips. I try to be patient as she talks and talks. "Mrs..?" I try, but no, she keeps on talking, "I can't understand a word of what you just said", I talk with loud voice – Too loud – I know, but I'm trying to make myself clear. That's when the woman starts to stare at me with mixed impression.

"I'm sorry to interrupt you but I haven't been able to understand anything you've been trying to tell me for I can't see your lips", I tell her with much calmer and lighter voice.
"I am so sorry", she apologizes.
"Not as sorry as I am", I say back, "Now, can you please start from the beginning?" – And she does.

I'm under a work desk to connect the wires and all when I see someone's legs next to me. I look up and see an older man; on his near forties or fifties looking back at me.

”So – You're the guy who talks with his hands?” the man asks.

”That's one way to put it”, I admit to him.

”So you talk?” he wonders.

”Yes. I am not a mute” I reply. How I don't like these questions.

”Can I help you somehow?” I offer.

”You are already doing what I asked you to do”, man tells me with a smile that reminds me off a fat cat that has catch a mouse but is too lazy to eat it.

”Well.. I guess I get back to work then”, I say to him while I get back under the desk. While I'm under the table I can see his chest moving – He's speaking to someone. I can catch him pointing at me few times. I'm distracted from my work while trying to fight against my own thoughts about him and my urge to ask what was wrong with him. I needed to hold my tongue if I wished to put bread on the table.

I'm more than happy when I get out of my personal hell. I text Jasper that I wouldn't go back there – Ever.

Should have taken the stairs

I look at huge building in front of me. Why does small companies want to get their retails to be in this kind of buildings? They're old and most of them don't have upgraded phonelines that would work with their technological equipment's and all the sudden I should be the magical wizard who can make it work? Yes – I can do it work for you after I have bought hundreds of different tools to make it work.. Seriously guys, do your homework. You can't assume that building from the - 50's with no renovations can have things that you need nowadays. What am I doing? Forget what I just said – I can use the extra money from your own stupidity.

I walk to the lobby. It's not one of those lobbies where there would be a person to guide you to the right place. This one has two plants in front of windows and a row of chairs. There's huge board with names of the companies that are present in the building. Then there's stairs and an elevator. The place I'm going is on the seventeenth floor. I could walk there, but then I'd be all sweaty and more or less light headed, for I have lots of things to carry along with me. Therefore, I decide to use the elevator.

I press the number seventeen twice and I'm about to leave when the doors get closed and the number screen shows the 'Up'-symbol. Elevator starts to move with weird, kind of dragging pace. It moves quite nicely to the number 'Eleven' when it suddenly makes odd, jumpy movement and lights run off for a second. I fell down because of it. The number screen shows bizarre looking picture. I can't feel any movement. I press the bell icon from the number board and take my phone. I start to text to Jasper.

Trapped in the elevator.

Could you call to this number?

(Me)

I take a picture of the sticker that has a number where you should call when the elevator is broken and sit down.

What in the World?!

Made the call, help is on it's way

Also called to the client.

They understand that you are late.

/Jasper

I text back:

*They better understand, for I'm stuck on **their** elevator.*

I should have taken the stairs..

Jasper responds way faster this time:

That's nice and YES!!!

You'll take the stairs always after you get out from there

/Jasper

I get back up and go in front of the mirror. I point at the screen which should show you the floor number; it only shows lines now and take a picture of me and text to my wife:

Got stuck in the elevator I guess..

(Me)

Are you serious?

/Delilah

I hardly come up with this good jokes..

(Me)

The elevator lights blicker once again and I fell down as the elevator tries to move. I press the bell button again; shouldn't it make the emergency brakes turn on or something, I think to myself.

In case this elevator manages to fall down..
I'd like you to know;
I love you
(Me)

I try to see if I could get out, for I start to panic, but
then my phone vibrates;

I love you too
I'm sure help is on it's way.
What happened?
/Delilah

I don't know.
(Me)

You poor thing.
Stay down.
You'll get out of there Matt, don't worry
/Delilah

This will be the last time I go to the elevator
(Me)

She sends me a laughing face.

Still;
Better you than me!

/Delilah

I agree with that. Thought of Delilah being trapped in elevator makes me feel sick. I use my 'spare-time' on my advantage to arrange my equipment's – I hate to admit that they're usually out of order. As I sit on the floor of the elevator my mind starts to wonder.

I can assure you one thing:
Reading the statistics of how many people ***have died*** in the elevator..
Well let's just say it isn't the best thing to do to calm your mind..

I'm lying on the floor when my phone starts vibrating again. I take it out of my pocket and see that Lucian, my brother, was calling a video call. I decline the call and text instead;

What do you want?
He replies much faster than I would have normally expected:

I'm at the doctors or something..
I really want to tell you something F2F.

I hated when he used 'teenage'-terms but then again it was mater of taste on these things. I call him instead. First thing I see are his red eyes.

"*Lucian – What's wrong?!*" I demand.

"*Police took me to the E.R today after I injured myself at some gas station..*" he signs. He is crying.

"*What? What is it?*"

"*I don't really know – *", he blurts. I'm in shock.

"*Lucian, what is wrong?!*" I try to aid him – Or me, I have no idea which one.

"*Can you come over?*" he asks.

"*I'm stuck in elevator*", I admit as I show him my surroundings.

"*Jees – Please come over here!!*", he begs.

I wait for him to calm down.

"*If I could, I would right away, but like I said; I AM STUCK. As soon as I get out of here I come to you, OK?*" I tell him.

"*You promise?*" he asks.

"*I promise*", I tell him back.

"*I'm so scared.. I – I don't know what to do, or say*", Lucian trembles.

"*I know.. Don't think about it now*", I calm him. I talk with him to the point that my battery dies and I don't even care. I only wanted to see my brother on that burning second.

After some time; The elevator starts to move again. Then the doors are opened. I sigh out of relief. There's three men waiting for me, they have a paper which is asking
"You OK?".
"I am alright", I tell them as I get out of the elevator with my bag. They start to talk to me with hyper-speed.
"I can't read your lips when you're talking that fast", I inform them, "Yet you don't have to speak super-slow.. Normal pace is fine", I add. They look at me with surprised impression.
"We are sorry that you were trapped in there", one of them apologizes.
"It's OK – I need to go now. I have emergency at home", I say as I go to the stairway with my case. Regardless how heavy my bag was – I was taking the stairs.

I was going to see Lucian.

Lucian Positive

Lucian was with his interpreter when I arrived to the hospital.

"Anything new?" I ask as I sign as well, "I'm his brother Matt". Lucian and interpreter share a look with each other.

"It doesn't look that good. They've run all kinds of tests and all.. Your parents are in the hall with the doctors", interpreter tells me while Lucian weeps.

"What – What did they find? What is going on?" I demand as policemen come to us.

"It's OK, I'm his brother", I tell them as they are trying to shoo me away.

"Are you a lawyer of some sort?" policeman asks.

"No, I'm his emergency contact number one", before I get to finish there's a huge mess. Lucian is the first one to raise his hand up. I watch him as he 'speaks' while interpreter starts to talk.

"Matt is the only person one the planet who still wants to back me up even I'm a low-life black sheep piece of shit. Could you mind us for a minute or two?

I've been waiting for him to come like two hours?!" he asks.

"My brother is sick and he wanted me here.. Is there something I should know?" I explain. Policemen scratch their hairlines but leave us alone.

"What happened -Why are you here?", I ask as I try to get the picture right.

"I was at the gas station", Lucian starts I can see that he is trying to make up a lie.

*"The **truth**, Lucian"*, I demand.

"I was going to buy some – OK? Next thing I knew my leg didn't support me and I fell to the ground.. Next thing I remember was being here", Lucian tells me. Interpreter nods at me to confirm his words.

"What's wrong with your leg?", I ask. Then I remember him having troubles with it for some time already. He had been limping for ages now.

"It has acted weird lately – Nothing much", Lucian belittles. I can see that he was sweating.

"You did go to see the doctor before, right?" I want to know. I had given him money to do so, even I knew it was always risky to give him any money.

"*I did. I just needed to leave while waiting for the results and my phone at the time went missing*", he tells me with apologetic look. I pat him on his shoulder to comfort him.

Mom and dad comes to the room. I can see that they've been crying. Interpreter leaves us for a minute. It was no point to have him there since we were all speaking the same language.

"*What is it?*" Lucian asks. Dad takes a deep breath before he can stop himself from shaking.

"*Doctors – They believe you may have ALS*"

"*Wait, my needles are always clean - !*" Lucian freaks.

"*Not AIDS, you dummy, **ALS**!*", I correct him, "*What's that?*" I ask then from my parents. Somehow the letters seemed familiar but my brains were rejecting to think anything clearly.

"*Amyotrophic lateral sclerosis*", my dad tries to clarify.

"*So.. What pills or shots shall I take to take care of it?*" Lucian asks. Mom breaks out in tears. Dad turns to look at him with tears in his eyes too.

"*There isn't any*", he tells him back.

Lucian's impression shifts.

"*Wait.. There's no cure?*" he asks in panic.

"*No*", my dad answers while mom takes his other hand. I sit down on one of the chairs because I feel like I might fall down.

"*Doctors are still running few tests to make sure of it, but they seemed pretty certain*" mom signs with her shaky hands.

"*What does it mean?*" Lucian asks.

"*That they haven't given a diagnose yet, but if it is ALS.. What happened today is only beginning of something worse*", Dad breaks the news for him.

"*What?*" I ask, but none of them even notice me.

I take my phone out of my pocket (which I had charged in my car a bit) and search for the mysterious 'ALS'. Tears escape my eyes. I hand my phone to Lucian.

"**No -NO!**" he cries. He looks at us like we would be joking but then his brighter mind knew we weren't. That's when the nurse came in to give him something that looked like a green goo. It was his doze of drugs, I knew. I had seen this before. As a drug-addict he was to be kept in drugs, he couldn't stop them right away or else he could die.

"*I wish you would stop using*", I sign weakly as I get my phone back.

"*Don't tell me what to do!*" Lucian hisses. Great, the stuff was kicking in more effectively this time.

"*I'm not.. I was simply making a wish*", I tell him back. I can see his impression shift into something I don't like. Lucian was slowly allowing himself being taken to the land where nothing mattered and he was the king of it. Too bad that his body was still locked here with us and every action he did had opposite action of response. I excused myself and left them to go home.

. . .

I stare myself at my bathroom mirror with an itch to hit my reflection. Why was it so hard to stay away from my brother? Why couldn't I turn my back to him and stop watching him to hurt himself? Why I needed to care about him?

"*Has the results came yet?*" Delilah asks as she comes to the bathroom. I nod at him. I hadn't been able to open the text message yet.

"*Do you want me to read it?*"

"*No.. I have to do it myself*", I disagree.

I go to the bedroom and take my phone from the night-stand. I open the text message and read the words over and over again. I realize that I'm crying. My legs betray me and I fall down. I feel Delilah's hand surrounding me. I try to hand her the phone so she can read the news too but she doesn't need the phone – She already knows by my reaction what the results were.

So she keeps holding me together when I was about to fall in pieces.

. . .

After a short day at work I decide to go to see my brother in the hospital again.

"*So ALS it is*", I say to him as I sit on the edge of the bed.

"*This sucks – I don't want to die*", Lucian curses.

"*Mister Hawking – The professor you used to like had ALS*" I tell him.

"*He did?*" Lucian asks.

"*He did*" I swear while nurse comes in and hands green goo to Lucian. I turn to look away to not show my disgust.

I feel a tap on my hand. I turn around.

"*I want you to forgive me Matt*", Lucian tells me with weak impression.

"*I won't forgive you*", I tell him back.

"*You have to!*" Lucian commands.

"*No – I don't*", I tell him back, "*Just because you're dying.. It doesn't mean that I need to forgive you for everything you have done. Or everything you didn't do! I asked many times for you to stop! Many times I tried to help you! Yet you always acted like an selfish asshole. Like it was your privileged to be the way you were – !*" I speed sign.

Lucian stares at me with tired look in his eyes – Which was odd. For usually his doze made him cheery.

"*It's not up to you to punish me of any of the things I did or didn't do. I'm asking for your forgiveness Matt. I am sorry. I am sorry I didn't change. I'm sorry for what I did and what I didn't. I* can't take any of it back now – Apparently I haven't got time to take it all back. You have to forgive me in order for yourself to move on.. Don't hold Grudge", Lucian reasons me.

"*I don't want to forgive you*", I tell him back before I leave.

Fairyland

It takes only three months for Lucian's health to crash down totally. Because of my grudge I was unable to go to see him and eventually he died alone. After his funeral Dodo started to act like he'd be leaving us soon too.

On one night.

I look at Dodo who's looking back at me with his gentle eyes. He puts his head on to my lap, glances at Delilah and then returns his gaze back at me. I tap at Delilah who looks at me with tired eyes.
"Dodo wants to say goodbye", I tell her. In an instant she is wide awake. I go to retrieve a blanket from the living room and I place the blanket on the floor and help Delilah to lift the heavy dog on to it. Delilahs eyes are wet, but she isn't crying just yet.
"Can you wake Rose too?" she asks. I nod at her and pet Dodo's head a bit before leaving.

Rose is sleeping with such peace that I feel bad for waking her up, but then again I knew she'd never

forgive me if she'd miss Dodo's farewell. So I sit next
to her and tap her twice.

"Rose?" I call her. She opens her heavy lids with
question as I wait.

"Dad?" she asks in confusion.

"Dodo wants to say goodbye", I tell her.

"What?" I repeat it twice more before she gets up.

"But where is he going?" Rose asks.

"To Heaven", I explain – Even I'm not quite sure would
dogs go there.. I assumed they did.

"Why? I don't want him to go", Rose wonders.

"It's his time to go", I explain to her as I take her into
my arms and go to the dog who's waiting.

Dodo waves his tale twice when he spots us,
but he's tired.

He doesn't have the strength to lift his head any longer.

I put Rose next to him and we all pet the dog.

He seems so pleased and happy to be surrounded by us.

Rose tells me that the window is open and fairies were
playing their music to Dodo.

I'm the first one to brake into tears.

"I know you must go.. I don't want you to.. but I forgive you", I tell to the dog's resting body.
"I forgive you" I tell him again and again before I can't move at all. I just cry.

"Forgive me for not forgiving you".

About 'Silence and Wind Chime'

. . .

This book is purely fiction. Any similarity to the real world is purely random coincidence.

. . .

This was my first novel-collection. It was weird for me too. But I had a feeling that these short stories were meant to be read like this. There is no use to force the story into a mold where it doesn't fit. So instead of one story I gave you three.

Thanks to..

- I'd like to thank my family – I love you!
- My cats and other friends from animal kingdom.
- I thank my friends. You have showed me what a true friendship is.
- Fans, without you reading, I wouldn't be able to pursue my dream.

...

As always:
Thank you for reading.